P9-CCS-021

7601 0100 559 957 4

Stories with Character

Enough to Go Around
A Story of Generosity

Kristin Johnson

illustrated by **Hannah Wood**

MILLBROOK PRESS • MINNEAPOLIS

To Ben Nelson —K.J.

For Mum and Dad. Who were generous enough to bring me up somewhere safe with someone good. —H.W.

Text and illustrations copyright © 2018 by
Lerner Publishing Group, Inc.

All rights reserved. International copyright secured. No part
of this book may be reproduced, stored in a retrieval system,
or transmitted in any form or by any means—electronic,
mechanical, photocopying, recording, or otherwise—without the
prior written permission of Lerner Publishing Group, Inc., except
for the inclusion of brief quotations in an acknowledged review.

Millbrook Press
A division of Lerner Publishing Group, Inc.
241 First Avenue North
Minneapolis, MN 55401 USA

For reading levels and more information, look up this title at
www.lernerbooks.com.

Main body text set in Slappy Inline 22/28.
Typeface provided by T26.

Library of Congress Cataloging-in-Publication Data

Names: Johnson, Kristin F., 1968– author. | Wood, Hannah,
    illustrator.
Title: Enough to go around : a story of generosity / by Kristin
    Johnson ; Illustrated by Hannah Wood.
Description: Minneapolis : Millbrook Press, [2018] | Series:
    Cloverleaf Books—stories with character | Summary: When
    Kevin learns that not everyone has enough to eat, like the
    full meals he enjoys with his family every night, he organizes
    a food drive at school. | Includes bibliographical references
    and index.
Identifiers: LCCN 2017005929 (print) | LCCN 2017033293
    (ebook) | ISBN 9781512498240 (eb pdf) |
    ISBN 9781512486483 (lb : alk. paper)
Subjects: | CYAC: Food banks—Fiction. | Generosity—Fiction. |
    Schools—Fiction.
Classification: LCC PZ7.1.J624 (ebook) | LCC PZ7.1.J624 Eno 2018
    (print) | DDC [E]—dc23

LC record available at https://lccn.loc.gov/2017005929

Manufactured in the United States of America
1-43472-33212-6/29/2017

TABLE OF CONTENTS

Chapter One

A Lunchroom Problem

Hi, I'm Kevin! Lunch is my favorite part of the day. Today we're talking about what we had for dinner last night.

"My grandma made chicken soup!" I say.

"My dad made spaghetti," Olivia shares.

"We ordered pizza," Jayden tells us.

Michael doesn't say anything. He looks down at the table.

What could be wrong?

An Even Bigger Problem

That night I tell my grandma what happened.

"Maybe Michael didn't know what to say,"
Grandma says. "Not everyone has enough to eat."

"In some families," Grandma explains,
"there just isn't enough to go around."

Everyone Pitches In

In class, I share my idea. "We should have a food drive!" My classmates volunteer to help.

Mrs. Mason says, "You all have generosity in your hearts."

We paint signs and make flyers about the food drive.

At a food drive, people donate food for others who need it.

Michael and I post the signs around school.

Olivia and other students take flyers to their families.

Chapter Four

The Food Drive

The next week, Grandma lets me pick out food to donate for the food drive.

I choose corn, pasta, and spaghetti sauce.
"My favorite foods!" I say.

At school, people put donations into boxes.

Jayden brings cans of soup. Olivia brings in diapers.

A food drive donation can be other items of need, not just food!

Chapter Five

Special Delivery

Michael and I help Grandma bring everything to the food shelf. **Michael is coming over to our house for dinner tonight!**

"That's a lot of food!" I say.

A food shelf may also be called a food pantry or food bank.

"Yes," Grandma says. "Today there is enough to go around."

Where Does Food Come From?

Brainstorm a list of all the places where food comes from. This could include grocery stores, farms, farmers' markets, restaurants, your kitchen, food shelves, and other places. Then draw a picture of a place where people get food in your community.

GLOSSARY

donate: to give something to a charity or special cause

enough: the right amount of something

food drive: a charity event in which people donate food and other items to people in need

food shelf: a place where people can get food and personal care items when they don't have money to buy them. A food shelf may also be called a food pantry or food bank.

generosity: an act of willingly giving to or sharing with others

volunteer: to offer to do something without getting paid

BOOKS

Johnson, Kristin. *In Your Shoes: A Story of Empathy.* Minneapolis: Millbrook Press, 2018. Read this story about a girl who learns the importance of considering other people's feelings.

Martin, Jacqueline Briggs. *Farmer Will Allen and the Growing Table*. Bellevue, WA: Readers to Eaters, 2013. Learn the story of Will Allen and his idea for sharing food within his community.

Shepherd, Jodie. *Kindness and Generosity: It Starts with Me.* New York: Children's Press, 2016. Read this book to see examples of kids showing kindness in real situations.

WEBSITES

Generation No Kid Hungry
https://generationnokidhungry.org/
Visit this website to learn more about the No Kid Hungry program, and read stories of other young people who are working to end hunger in America.

Kind Spring
http://www.kindspring.org/ideas/
Check out these lists of ideas for other ways to be generous through good deeds.